» ATTENTION, READER

Princess Leia of Alderaan and Luke Skywalker
are two of the galaxy's greatest rebels
– but they need your help!

This book is full of choices – choices that
lead to different adventures, choices that
you must make to help Luke and Leia.

Do not read the following pages straight through
from start to finish! When you are asked to make
a choice, follow the instructions to see where
that choice will lead Luke and Leia next.

CHOOSE CAREFULLY.

AND MAY THE FORCE BE WITH YOU!

A LONG TIME AGO
IN A GALAXY FAR, FAR AWAY. . . .

LUKE SKYWALKER SENSED the attack a second before Commander Narra's warning crackled over the comm.

"Red Squadron – we have incoming. Multiple fighters, moving in fast."

Luke threw his X-wing into a sharp roll as emerald plasma bolts shot past his cockpit.

"That was close, Red Five," Narra scolded him. *"Too close."*

Luke scowled as he levelled out. Arhul Narra had taken command of Red Squadron soon after the Battle of Yavin and had made it abundantly clear that Luke wouldn't get special treatment. He wasn't kidding. The grizzled commander always seemed to be on Luke's back, demanding more of him than anyone else, including Wedge Antilles, who had flown with Luke against the Death Star.

"You okay?" Wedge asked over the comm, bringing his own X-wing alongside Luke's.

"What was that?" Luke asked in response, searching the nebula for any sign of whoever had attacked him.

From his position behind Luke, R2-D2 burbled a reply.

"A TIE fighter?" Luke asked the droid. "Are you sure?"

"I only caught a glimpse before it disappeared back into the cloud," Wedge said, *"but it was like no TIE I've ever seen."*

Another voice joined the conversation. It was Jamman, a Duros pilot who had recently joined the squadron. *"Could they be experimental models?"*

"Whatever they are, keep your eyes sharp," Narra replied. *"They could be anywhere in all this dust."*

"Copy that, Red Leader," Jamman acknowledged.

Narra was right. Red Squadron was accompanying the *Nema*, an Alliance transport carrying essential medical supplies. The Imperial Navy would stop at nothing to bring down such a valuable resource, so the Alliance Council had plotted a course through the Kiax nebula. Most spacefarers avoided the cloud of thick, swirling space dust, as it wreaked havoc on their sensor readings. Mon Mothma, the Alliance's chief of state, had gambled they'd be able to use it to slip past the Empire unnoticed, but what if she'd been wrong?

Luke felt a tug at his mind and recognised it immediately as the Force, the mysterious energy field that connected all living things. Luke had felt it all his

2

life but hadn't known its true power, not until he met
Ben Kenobi.

"They're coming back," he muttered.

"How do you know?" Wedge asked.

Ahead of them, two ships appeared through the
sea of whirling dust. Luke could see what Wedge had
meant. The Empire had dozens of different TIEs, from
the standard fighter to the advanced model Darth
Vader had flown during the Battle of Yavin. Yet they
were all constructed along similar lines, with the same
gunmetal colour scheme.

These were different. The TIE on the right was
bright blue with three curved wings, while the fighter
on the left was yellow, its wings long and pointed, with
a large cannon where the cockpit should be.

Both had opened fire.

Luke and Wedge peeled apart, the energy beams
passing harmlessly between them.

"Fighter on your tail, Red Five," Jamman reported as
Luke ducked and weaved.

"Thanks, Red Three."

Luke reached out with the Force, seeing a flash of
blue in his mind's eye. The TIE with the three wings.

He pulled up, throwing his X-wing into a loop. R2
squealed in protest as they soared over their pursuer,
dropping down behind so the hunter became the hunted.

3

Luke didn't need his targeting computer. He pressed down on his trigger and ripped the TIE fighter apart.

Luke didn't have time to celebrate. He could feel something was wrong. Slamming his X-wing into a sharp turn, he raced back towards the *Nema*. Jamman was in trouble, unable to shake the yellow TIE fighter with the heavy cannon.

"Red Three, look out!"

Luke's warning came a moment too late. The cannon discharged and Jamman's X-wing exploded in a blaze of superheated metal.

"No!" Luke cried out, destroying the yellow fighter with a barrage of ruby-red lasers.

Above him, Wedge was caught in a dogfight with yet another TIE fighter, this one painted red and sporting a single wing positioned like a sand shark's fin.

"Could do with some assistance, Red Five..."

"I've got you," Luke said, pulling up. The TIE was so focused on Wedge that it didn't even see Luke coming until it was too late. The strange starfighter erupted in a ball of crimson flame.

"Thanks."

"Not a problem," Luke told Wedge.

Meanwhile, Narra was exchanging shots with a green TIE fighter with S-foils instead of solar wings, and Red Four – a Twi'lek pilot named Elar – was flying straight towards a purple fighter with a cockpit shaped like a bullet.

"Need a hand, Red Four?" Wedge asked, only to get a swift rebuttal from the female pilot.

"Everything's under control, Red Two. Unless you want to see how it's done?"

But before Elar could display her marksmanship, the purple TIE peeled off into the nebula.

"Where'd he go?" Elar asked.

"Looks like you scared him off," Wedge replied.

Above them, Narra's opponent had also escaped.

"We can't let them get away!" Luke shouted.

"Let them go, Red Five," Narra told him. *"Our first duty is to protect the transport."*

"But what if there's an entire armada in there?" Luke argued. "We'll never know unless we follow them."

"Protect the transport," came the stern reply.

WHAT DOES LUKE DO?

STAY WITH THE TRANSPORT – GO TO PAGE 25.
GO AFTER THE TIE FIGHTERS – TURN TO PAGE 20.

LEIA SHOOK HER HEAD. "We can't ignore this."

"Nor can we risk further ships on a rescue mission. For all we know, the *Nema* has been destroyed."

"But—"

"The decision has been made," Mon Mothma said, and it was clear that the conversation was over.

"Commander Narra, if I may have a word . . ."

When the chief of state and the commander left, Luke gave Leia a weak smile and went to follow them out, but Leia touched his arm to stop him. She leaned close to Luke, her voice low.

"We can't leave it like this."

"What else can we do? You heard Mon Mothma. She's made her decision."

"And it's wrong," Leia insisted. "Those medical supplies are too important to abandon. If Mon Mothma won't authorise a rescue mission, then we'll just have to go ourselves."

DOES LUKE AGREE TO HELP LEIA?

YES - TURN TO PAGE 58.

NO - GO TO PAGE 32.

"WHAT DO WE DO?" Luke asked.

Leia switched off the comlink. "We need to find the *Nema*."

"But the distress call . . ." he began.

"Luke, the supplies on the transport could save thousands of people."

He could tell that this was hard for her, so Luke took the *Falcon* to the *Nema*'s last known position.

The transport was nowhere to be seen, just like before. Luke even reached out with the Force, but he felt nothing but regret.

"It's useless," Leia finally admitted. "We should check on that ship."

But the distress call had ceased.

"Perhaps they got away," Luke suggested.

"Or were destroyed," Leia said quietly, pressing controls on the navicomputer. "Course set for home."

They would return to the fleet empty-handed.

THE END

**CAN YOU GO BACK AND HELP LUKE AND
LEIA MAKE BETTER CHOICES?**

"LEIA, YOU CAN'T," Luke told her. "Not after everything Han's done for us . . ."

"You said you would help me."

"Not like this."

"Then you don't have to." She turned and marched towards the turbolift.

"Leia, wait—"

He watched helplessly as the lift doors closed and she was whisked away.

WHAT DOES LUKE DO?

TELL HAN - TURN TO PAGE 12.

HOPE THAT LEIA CHANGES HER MIND - GO TO PAGE 22.

"COULD THAT BE THE *NEMA*?" Leia asked.

"I don't know," Luke said, turning to R2. "Can we lock on to the signal?"

R2-D2's probe whirled in the access port, but there was too much interference.

Luke closed his eyes and focused on the voice calling for help.

"What are you doing?"

"Just trust me," he told Leia, guiding the *Falcon* where the Force led him.

Flashes burst above the cockpit and the ship shuddered. Luke's eyes snapped open as a starfighter streaked past. "It's one of the TIEs."

The bizarre fighter was heading towards a badly damaged craft floating in the middle of the nebula. The TIE fired again, its blasts only just missing the ravaged vessel.

The *Falcon* shook as two more TIEs roared past.

"You fly," Luke said, jumping up. "I'll take the cannons."

Minutes later, he was sitting in his usual gun turret

as Leia brought them about. His first shot found its target, reducing a TIE with four stubby wings to dust.

As one, the other three fighters broke off their attack and fled into the nebula.

WHAT DO THEY DO?

CHASE THE TIE FIGHTERS - TURN TO PAGE 34.

HELP THE DAMAGED SHIP - GO TO PAGE 42.

LATER THAT EVENING, Leia watched C-3PO deliver a message to Han and Chewie. The protocol droid convinced Han that he was needed in the briefing room.

Once they had left, Leia hurried onto the *Falcon*.

"I can't believe you're going through with this."

Luke was waiting for her in the belly of the ship.

"Luke, there's nothing left to discuss—" she began.

"I wouldn't say that."

Han Solo strode up the ramp towards her.

Leia glared at Luke. "You told him?"

Luke shrugged. "I had to. It's too dangerous."

"And I thought we were friends," Han said, trying to make light of the situation.

"So did I," Leia said, barging past the smuggler so no one could see the tears in her eyes.

What had she been thinking?

THE END

**CAN YOU GO BACK AND HELP LUKE AND
LEIA MAKE BETTER CHOICES?**

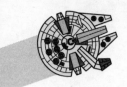

"CAPTAIN SOLO?"

Han Solo groaned as C-3PO bustled up to the *Millennium Falcon.*

"Not now, Goldenrod," he said, not looking up from his repairs.

"I'm afraid I really must talk to you."

"We're busy," Han said, activating a bit driver to drown out the protocol droid's voice. "See? This is us, being busy."

The fussy robot pressed on regardless. "But I have an urgent message from Princess Leia. She sent me to fetch you without delay."

"Chewie, tell Threepio we're not coming."

The Wookiee barked a none-too-subtle warning.

"Well, there's no need to shoot the messenger," C-3PO commented testily.

"No, but I *could* remove both his legs," Han said, waving his bit driver in the droid's general direction.

C-3PO finally took the hint and tottered away. "Oh, dear. The princess is going to be *most* disappointed. She so wanted to warn you about Jabba the Hutt."

The mention of his former employer caught Han's interest. "What about him?"

C-3PO paused. "According to our contact on Tatooine, Jabba has increased the bounty on your head to something in the region of a million credits."

A grin spread across Han's face. "A million? Did you hear that, Chewie? Not bad, huh?"

But that wasn't all.

"Indeed. And according to our intel, the bounty for your companion is two million."

"*Two* million?" Han repeated, visibly shocked.

"No way is the fuzzball worth twice as much as me."
He raised his hands as Chewbacca towered over him,
bellowing in protest. "Hey, I'm just saying, pal. *I'm* the
one with the reputation, not you."

"Perhaps there's been a mistake," C-3PO said, heading
towards the turbolift. "I'm sure the princess will explain."

"She better," Han said, ushering his hairy companion
after the droid. "Come on, you big lug. Something about
this isn't right!"

He was still shaking his head when the turbolift doors
closed. "Two million. Unbelievable."

"Like taking clams from a Gungan," Leia muttered as she emerged from her hiding place behind the *Falcon*.

"You're enjoying this, aren't you?" said Luke as she hurried up the ramp.

"No," she insisted, although her grin told him otherwise.

Soon they were standing in the familiar confines of the freighter's shabby cockpit. Luke hesitated by Han's chair as Leia dropped into the co-pilot's seat.

"Hurry up. They'll be back soon."

Shaking his head, Luke sat down and primed the *Falcon*'s systems. "Are you *sure* you want to do this?"

"We don't have any choice," Leia replied, feeding the nebula's coordinates into the navicomputer.

C-3PO's voice crackled from the comlink she had strapped to her jacket.

"Princess? This is See-Threepio. Where are you? I have Captain Solo with me as requested but can't find you anywhere."

Luke frowned. "Han won't wait for long."

"Then let's get going," Leia said, indicating the starfield beyond the bay doors.

Luke fired the repulsors, but nothing happened.

Leia looked at him expectantly. "Aren't we supposed to be moving?"

Luke jabbed buttons, but nothing was working.

16

"She won't take off. The engines are online, but she's not responding."

Leia let out an exasperated breath. "Does nothing on this grease bucket work?"

Luke activated the ship's fault locator. "Everything's working perfectly. The *Falcon* is just . . . frozen."

On the comlink, C-3PO was pleading with the smugglers to stay with him until he had located the princess.

"Then unfreeze it," Leia snapped. "They're coming back."

Behind them, R2-D2 gave an agitated bleep. Luke swivelled in his chair. "An immobiliser? Are you sure?"

R2 blooped a response.

"Does an immobiliser do what I *think* it does?" Leia asked.

Luke stared at the controls in despair. "It means that only Han and Chewie can launch the *Falcon*."

Leia shook her head. "It's like they don't trust us."

"Can you blame them?" Luke said as C-3PO reported that Han and Chewbacca were returning to the hangar bay.

Leia turned to R2. "Can you override the code?"

The astromech thrust his probe into a socket as Luke glanced nervously at the turbolift. "Anytime now would be good. . ."

The squat droid gave a bleep of triumph, and the engines swelled.

"You did it!" Luke said, activating the repulsors.

"And just in time," Leia said as Han Solo strode into the hangar bay to witness his beloved ship sweeping out into the stars.

"What do you think is going to upset him more?" Luke asked as they entered the nebula. "That we stole his ship or that you lied about the bounty?"

"You're not helping, Luke," Leia said sullenly.

It was obvious she was feeling guilty, but it was too late. Luke felt the same. As soon as they'd cleared *Home One*, he'd wanted to swing back around, but as his Aunt Beru had always said, what was done was done.

Besides, for all his guilt, Luke was *really* enjoying piloting Han's ship. It was fair to say that it wasn't the smoothest of freighters. Even with the *Falcon*'s power and manoeuvrability, the engines occasionally seemed to fight *against* the flight stick rather than responding to its commands, as if the ship's systems had a will of their own. It was lucky that Luke had grown up flying thrown-together skyhoppers on Tatooine. Sitting in the pilot seat and wrestling with the ageing starship's controls almost felt like coming home.

"So where did you last see the *Nema*?" Leia asked.

Luke checked the displays. As expected, the space dust was wreaking havoc on the *Falcon*'s sensors.

"Somewhere around here, but I can't be certain."

He reached over to widen the sensor reach, and a voice burst out of the comlink.

"Help us, please. We're under attack."

DO THEY ANSWER THE DISTRESS CALL?

YES - TURN TO PAGE 10.

NO. THEY MUSTN'T GET DISTRACTED - GO TO PAGE 8.

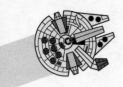

LUKE'S HANDS TIGHTENED around his flight stick. "They can't have gone far. I'm going after them."

Gunning his engines, he dove deeper into the nebula.

"You better be right about this," came a familiar voice over the comm. Luke glanced to his right and saw Wedge dropping into position beside him.

"Because if you're wrong, Narra is going to have us cleaning fuel lines for a month," Elar added, drawing up on his left.

Luke smiled. The rest of Red Squadron believed in him, even if their commander didn't.

"So, where are they?" Wedge asked.

A message from R2 scrolled across Luke's screen. He frowned.

"Yeah, I know the sensors are offline," he told the droid. "But I can still find them."

He tried reaching out with the Force, but for once Wedge was one step ahead.

"I see them," Wedge said. *"And that's not all."*

The dense cloud had thinned to reveal the fleeing

TIE fighters streaking towards an asteroid field. Almost as quickly as they had appeared, the TIEs plunged into the tumbling rocks, disappearing from sight.

"I'm going in," Luke told the others.

"Into the asteroids?" Elar said. *"You'll never make it out in one piece!"*

DOES LUKE LISTEN TO ELAR?

**YES. THE ASTEROID BELT WILL BE TOO
DANGEROUS - GO TO PAGE 41.
NO. HE CAN'T LET THE TIE FIGHTERS
ESCAPE - TURN TO PAGE 36.**

"YOU COULD HAVE warned me, kid!"

Luke looked up from his station on *Home One's* flight deck.

"Warned you about what?" he asked Han, knowing full well what the answer would be.

"Leia took the *Falcon*. Don't tell me you didn't know."

There was no point denying it. "I tried to stop her."

"Tried to stop who?" someone asked calmly. Mon Mothma was standing behind them.

Han jabbed a finger at the chief of state. "Your precious princess has stolen my ship."

"And taken it where?" Mon Mothma asked.

Luke rose to his feet. "The nebula."

"She's looking for the *Nema*?"

He nodded.

Mon Mothma's face flushed. "And after I told her . . ." She swallowed the rest of the sentence and activated a comlink. "Commander Narra, scramble Red Squadron. You have a stolen ship to recover."

"*The* Nema?" Narra asked over the comm.

"No," Mon Mothma replied, her steely gaze fixed on Luke. "The *Millennium Falcon*."

She cut the communication and raised her eyebrows expectantly. "You heard the order, Lieutenant."

Luke hurried from the flight deck to join the rest of his squadron. Leia had really done it this time. Why hadn't he stopped her?

THE END

COULD LUKE AND LEIA HAVE MADE BETTER CHOICES? GO BACK AND FIND OUT.

LEIA LOOKED AS IF she was going to argue but stopped herself.

"You're right," she finally said. "It's just . . ."

"Sacrifices must be made," Mon Mothma told her. "We can't risk taking more ships into the nebula. Thank you, all."

Narra told Luke to report to the hangar bay. Luke nodded but hung back to speak to Leia.

"I'm sorry we lost the transport. I know the supplies were important."

"You did what you thought was right." She looked at the large star map at the back of the briefing room.

"Leia?"

She sighed. "I can't help thinking that we shouldn't have given up so easily. There's something in that nebula, but . . ."

"But we have our orders," Luke reminded her.

"Exactly. So I'd better start looking for a new route."

THE END

COULD LUKE AND LEIA HAVE DONE THINGS DIFFERENTLY?
GO BACK AND FIND OUT.

LUKE SLUMPED IN HIS SEAT. Red Leader was right. Flying after the TIEs would leave the *Nema* vulnerable to attack.

"It's for the best," Wedge told Luke over the comm as he brought his X-wing alongside Narra's fighter.

"Copy that, Red Two," Luke admitted. "I just can't shake the feeling that there's something out there in the nebula. Something bad."

THE END

DO YOU THINK LUKE MADE THE RIGHT CHOICE?
GO BACK AND TRY AGAIN.

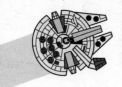

"MEDICAL TRANSPORTS do not simply
disappear, Commander," Mon Mothma said when they
had returned to the fleet.

Narra shifted uncomfortably beneath the chief
of state's steely gaze. The remaining members of Red
Squadron were standing in the briefing room on board
Home One, the Alliance's Mon Calamari flagship. Luke
could understand Narra's discomfort, especially as Leia
Organa was standing beside Mon Mothma.

"Do you think it was destroyed?" Leia asked.

"I wish I knew, Princess," Narra replied. "When we
returned from the asteroid field, it was nowhere to be
seen."

"And your sensors?" Mon Mothma asked.

"They were next to useless in the nebula," Luke
admitted.

"But why did you leave the *Nema* unattended in
the first place?" the chief of state asked, her voice
deceptively calm. "Your orders were to accompany the
transport at all times."

Luke felt his cheeks flush. "It was me," he blurted

out. "Red Leader told me to stay with the transport, but I went after the TIE fighters."

Mon Mothma's brow creased. "You disobeyed a direct order?"

"We all did," Wedge cut in, stepping forward, as did Elar.

"Lieutenant Antilles is correct," the purple-skinned Twi'lek confirmed. "We all disobeyed orders."

"And now another ship is lost," Mon Mothma said sternly.

Luke frowned. "*Another* ship? This has happened before?"

Mon Mothma dismissed them without answering the question.

Elar and Wedge made to leave, but Commander Narra held his ground, intrigued by the chief of state's comment. "I'm sorry, ma'am, but if there have been other disappearances . . ."

Mon Mothma exchanged glances with Leia before giving in.

"Very well. A total of three transports have been lost in the nebula."

"Taken by the Empire?" Luke asked, shocked by the revelation.

Mon Mothma turned her gaze to the large star map behind her. "There is no evidence of Imperial activity within the nebula."

"Other than the TIE fighters," Wedge pointed out.

"TIE fighters that, by your own report, varied considerably from known Imperial designs."

"Who else could it be?" Luke asked.

"Other forces use TIE fighters," Leia reminded him. "The Mining Guild . . . the Forgesmiths of Matterhelm . . ."

"Both of which are loyal to the Empire."

Mon Mothma raised a hand to silence him. "The fact of the matter is that the Kiax nebula is no longer safe. We must find alternate routes."

"And what about the missing ships?" Leia asked.

"We learn from our mistakes," the chief of state replied, "and ensure such risks are never taken again."

DOES LEIA AGREE WITH MON MOTHMA?

YES - TURN TO PAGE 24.

NO. THEY SHOULD FIND THE MISSING SHIPS - GO TO PAGE 7.

LUKE IGNORED THE VOICE in his head and plunged deeper into the asteroid field. R2 squealed sharply as the power couplings in the damaged S-foil ruptured, taking the entire wing with them. The X-wing spun out of control, spiralling towards a large asteroid.

Luke slammed his hand down on the ejector controls, and a face mask snapped down from his flight goggles. The canopy flipped away and the rocket beneath his seat fired, blasting him clear of the cockpit seconds before the X-wing ploughed into the asteroid.

The injector seat spluttered and failed, the booster running out of fuel. Luke drifted among the spinning space rocks, listening to the beep of the seat's automatic homing beacon. He called out as R2 tumbled past him, but there was no reply. The astromech had lost one of his legs, and his systems were offline.

Luke wasn't about to let R2 float into the void. Closing his eyes, he reached out with the Force and pulled the droid towards him. When R2 was close enough, Luke grabbed the astromech and held him tight.

"I'm sorry, buddy," he whispered to his dormant droid. "This is all my fault. I should've listened to everyone. I should have listened to Ben."

THE END

CAN YOU GO BACK AND HELP LUKE
MAKE A BETTER CHOICE?

"I DON'T KNOW," Luke said. "Heading out with a squadron of X-wings is one thing, but flying off on your own . . ."

"But I won't be alone, not if you're with me."

Luke hesitated, and Leia's expression hardened.

"Fine. You stay here; but I'm going."

Luke tried to stop her, but she stormed out of the briefing room.

"Leia, wait."

"There's nothing left to say," Leia told him as he caught up with her.

"What are you going to do? Take an X-wing? Pilot it yourself?"

"I don't see why not."

"It's not safe," he said, following Leia into a turbolift.

"Then I'll take Artoo," she said, punching the button for the hangar bay. "*He* won't let me down."

"I'm not letting you down. I'm just trying to stop you from doing something you might regret later."

"You're not going to change my mind," Leia told him as the turbolift doors opened. "I'm going back to that nebula no matter what you or Mon Mothma says."

"Is that right?" came a stern voice from the hangar bay. Leia turned to see Mon Mothma staring right at her.

"Mon Mothma. I was just . . ."

"Go to your quarters," the chief of state said quietly. "We'll talk later."

Leia opened her mouth to argue but knew this was a battle she wouldn't win.

THE END

CAN YOU GO BACK AND HELP LUKE AND LEIA MAKE BETTER CHOICES?

"WE CAN'T LET THEM GET AWAY!" Luke yelled into his headset.

"I hope you know what you're doing," Leia said as she brought the *Falcon* around.

So do I, Luke thought as he spotted the fleeing starfighters.

"That's it," Luke encouraged her. "Stay on them."

The *Falcon* shook as it was struck from above.

"What was that?"

"Someone's firing at us," Leia replied.

"More TIEs?"

There was another impact, harder this time. Those weren't lasers; they were torpedoes!

WHAT SHOULD THEY DO?

CONCENTRATE ON THE TIE FIGHTERS - TURN TO PAGE 66.

RETURN FIRE - GO TO PAGE 47.

LUKE IGNORED THE WARNING, closing his
S-foils and diving into the asteroid field.

R2 was quick to tell him *exactly* what he thought of
the manoeuvre.

"Just be quiet, will you?" Luke snapped. "I need to
concentrate."

Sweat was running down his face. He was no fool.
He knew this was dangerous.

Luke.

The voice made his breath catch.

It was Ben, cut down by Darth Vader – gone but
somehow always near. Ben would believe in him. Ben
would trust him.

Luke, you need to turn back. This is reckless.

No. Luke couldn't believe it. Even Ben doubted him.
He'd show them.

He'd show them all.

Ahead of him the green TIE fighter broke cover,
firing at a nearby asteroid. The strike set off a chain
reaction, asteroids bouncing off each other. Luke
banked to the right but clipped a tumbling rock. R2
wailed as the X-wing went into a spin, Luke wrestling

with the controls. It took everything he had just to pull up, but Luke wasn't finished yet. The TIE fighter was still out there. He *had* to find it.

Luke, Ben's voice urged, *no. Let it go.*

WHAT DOES LUKE DO?

LEAVE THE ASTEROID FIELD - TURN TO PAGE 38.

CONTINUE TO FOLLOW THE TIE

FIGHTER - TURN TO PAGE 30.

LUKE SIGHED. Ben was right. He'd never make it through the rest of the asteroids, not with a damaged wing.

He tried to guide his starfighter out of the fight, but energy bolts pummelled his bow. Luke looked up to see the TIE Elar had been fighting closing in at breakneck speed. There was nowhere for Luke to go. He was trapped.

Laser fire burst from above, buckling the TIE fighter's hull. The bullet-shaped spacecraft disintegrated, and Luke raised his hand to protect his eyes from the sudden glare.

An X-wing swooped down in front of him, and Commander Narra barked over the comm: *"Follow me out of the asteroids."*

Luke groaned but did as he was told, R2 bleeping in his ear.

"Yes, I know you told me not to do it," he replied. "You and everyone else."

Wedge and Elar fell into formation alongside him, following Red Leader back to the transport. No one spoke, although Luke didn't need the Force to feel the anger radiating from Narra's X-wing.

"That's not right," Narra finally said.

"Commander?" Wedge asked.

"The Nema," Narra replied. *"It's not at its last coordinates. It's … gone!"*

TURN TO PAGE 26.

LUKE COULDN'T BELIEVE what he was hearing. "You're going to steal the *Falcon*?"

"No, of course not," Leia replied, stepping into the lift pod. "I'm going to *borrow* it, and you're going to help."

Luke followed her in, and the doors shut behind him. "How?"

"We need a distraction, something to lure Han away from the ship."

"Like what?"

"Like one of the droids," Leia said, a plan starting to form.

WHICH DROID DO THEY SEND TO DISTRACT HAN?

R2-D2 - TURN TO PAGE 60.

C-3PO - GO TO PAGE 13.

"LISTEN TO RED FOUR," a voice rumbled through the comlink. Luke groaned. Narra had flown after them. Now Luke was in for it.

"Copy that, Red Leader," he said, pulling up on his stick.

"We'll talk about your insubordination when we return to the fleet," Narra told him as they flew back to the medical transport.

"Sir, I was just—"

"I know exactly what you were doing, and I won't stand for it, Death Star hero or ..."

His voice trailed off.

"Red Leader?"

"The t-transport," Narra stammered. *"It's ... gone."*

TURN TO PAGE 26.

"GO AFTER THEM!" Luke yelled into his headset, but Leia's response was firm.

"No, we need to help that ship. It looks like they're in real trouble."

She was right. Energy was surging along the battered ship's hull. It looked like it might explode at any moment.

By the time he'd made it back to the cockpit, Leia had brought the *Falcon* alongside the stricken craft and was trying to hail it.

"Unidentified vessel. We are here to help. Please respond."

The only response was a metal disk that shot from the ship to clamp on to the *Falcon*'s hull. The dashboard crackled, and every light on the ship blinked out in unison, plunging them into darkness.

"What happened?" Luke asked as R2 activated his spotlight.

Leia tried several of the instruments. "They've siphoned our power. Thrusters. Shields. Everything's gone."

"Not everything," Luke realised as the *Falcon* was yanked towards the smaller ship. "We still have gravity and life support. Whoever is on that ship is planning to come on board."

"Pirates?" Leia asked as a transparent boarding tube extended from the not-so-damaged cruiser.

WHAT DO THEY DO?

FIGHT THE PIRATES - TURN TO PAGE 70.

TRY TO TRICK THE PIRATES - GO TO PAGE 98.

BEHIND THEM, R2-D2 BLEEPED. The little droid was rocking on his feet, the deck plate beneath him creaking.

"I told you," Leia said, ushering the astromech off the grill. "Nooks and crannies."

She bent down and slipped her fingers through the grating, pulling hard. The deck plate came away to reveal one of the many secret compartments Han had installed around the ship. It would be a tight squeeze, but there was just enough room for all three of them to hide.

Luke jumped into the pit and helped R2 down behind him. Leia leapt in and pulled the grate over their heads.

Luke held his breath as two aliens stomped over the grate, heading towards the escape pods.

"There's no one here, Grox," the squid-faced Quarren reported into his comlink.

"*A pity,*" came the surly reply. "*The Tech Masters pay good creds for scavengers. Ah well. Let's get this crate back to Trionak.*"

Light streamed through the grate as power was

suddenly restored. Luke and Leia listened as the boarding tube disengaged and the raiders returned to the front of the ship.

"Where's Trionak?" Luke whispered after they had gone.

Leia shrugged. "Our destination, by the sounds of it."

"What about the immobiliser?" Luke asked.

"You had Artoo deactivate it, remember? Still, that's not such a bad thing. . ."

"Not bad?" Luke parroted. "We've just been hijacked!"

"Yes," she said patiently, waiting for him to get her meaning.

Luke's eyes went wide as he realised. "Like our missing ships!"

Leia nodded. "This could be our best chance of finding the *Nema*. For all we know, those pirates have just done us a favour."

TURN TO PAGE 72.

LEIA BROUGHT THEM AROUND, and a large cruiser swung into view. The ship was at least twice the size of the *Falcon*, its armoured hull bristling with weapons.

Luke gripped the firing controls. They wouldn't survive another attack. He would have to make his shot count.

WHAT SHOULD LUKE TARGET?

THE SHIP'S ENGINES - GO TO PAGE 52.

THE SHIP'S WEAPONS - TURN TO PAGE 50.

"NOT FOR LONG," Luke said, leaping from the ramp to race towards the slaves. His feet slipped on loose nuts and bolts, but his lightsaber hummed as it ignited.

The droid that had struck the slave turned but was too slow. Luke swung his saber in an arc, the glowing blade slicing through the droid's chest. The droid collapsed, its segmented body adding to the pile of scrap metal.

As the slaves huddled together, Luke rounded on the second droid. It pulled back its electro-whip to strike, but Luke swept low, removing the robot's feet. It tumbled back, and Luke plunged the saber into its chest plate.

He didn't hear the third and final droid reaching for its blaster. He didn't have to. He moved on instinct, blocking the laser bolt. Luke charged forward, but the green-painted droid was already under fire from Leia. Faced with two targets, the droid opted for the princess. It aimed but never got to pull the trigger. Luke's lightsaber flashed in front of its photoreceptors and its severed hand hit the ground, blaster still clutched in its metallic grip. Luke brought his saber around and cleaved the droid in two.

His heart hammering, Luke extinguished his lightsaber and turned to the slaves he had liberated.

"What did you do that for?" asked a painfully thin Sullustan who wore a thick stun collar around his scrawny neck.

"I rescued you," Luke said as Leia scrambled over to join them.

"No, you doomed us," said the human they'd seen whipped.

The Sullustan agreed. "The Tech Masters will dispatch a punishment squad."

WHAT DO LUKE AND LEIA SAY TO THE SLAVES?

"WHO ARE THE TECH MASTERS?" - TURN TO PAGE 106.
"WHY DON'T YOU FIGHT BACK?" - TURN TO PAGE 84.

LUKE FIRED, aiming for the ship's torpedo tubes. He scored a direct hit, but it wasn't enough. Turbolasers lanced towards them, slicing through the *Falcon's* shield. Explosions tore through the freighter as a sibilant voice hissed over the comm.

"Prepare to be boarded, Solo."

His guns dead, Luke scrambled up the ladder to find Leia already running for the escape pods.

"Come on!" she yelled, pulling him along. They each squeezed into a tiny life pod and shot out into the void. As they rocketed away, Luke took one last look at Han's beloved *Falcon*.

I'll get her back for you, he silently promised his friend, *even if it's the last thing I do.*

THE END

**CAN YOU GO BACK AND HELP LUKE AND
LEIA MAKE BETTER CHOICES?**

"YOU THINK WE haven't thought of that?" the Sullustan snapped. "Even if we could get the ships off the ground, the entire planet is surrounded by an impenetrable force field. Nothing gets in or out unless the Tech Masters allow it."

"Including transmissions?" Leia asked.

"You tried to call for help, didn't you?"

"Our droid couldn't get through," Leia said.

"Hardly surprising," the scaled alien told her. "Only one transmitter works."

"Let me guess," Luke said. "The one used by the Tech Masters."

The Rodian sighed. "Catch on quick, don't you?"

"But there must be a way to escape. There's always a way."

"Not here there isn't," the Sullustan insisted.

WHAT DO THEY DO?

LUKE ENCOURAGES THEM NOT TO GIVE UP SO EASILY - GO TO PAGE 101.

LEIA PROMISES TO HELP - TURN TO PAGE 85.

"GET BEHIND THEM!" Luke yelled. "I'm going to target their propulsion systems."

Leia threw the *Falcon* into a dizzying roll. The enemy ship was larger, but it was also slower. It started to turn, but Leia angled up, giving Luke a clear view of its ion thrusters. He mashed down on the triggers, and the quad cannon bucked in response.

The energy bolts slammed into the cruiser's engines, the resulting explosion tearing the vessel apart.

"You did it!" Leia cheered, looping through the debris, but Luke wasn't in the mood to celebrate. The TIE fighters would be long gone, and judging by the rattle of their engines, the *Falcon* had suffered considerable damage during the attack.

They'd have to return to *Home One*.

The smuggler wasn't going to be happy when he saw what they'd done to his ship – and all for nothing!

THE END

**CAN YOU GO BACK AND HELP LUKE AND
LEIA MAKE BETTER CHOICES?**

"THEY'RE ON BOARD," Leia said, skidding to a halt as she heard footsteps ahead. Luke's lightsaber was already in his hand.

Once again, Leia put a restraining hand on his arm. "Don't. It'll only tell them we're here."

Reluctantly, Luke let his arm drop. "Then where are we going to hide?"

WHERE SHOULD THEY HIDE?

IN HAN'S CABIN - TURN TO PAGE 75.

IN A SECRET COMPARTMENT - GO TO PAGE 44.

LEIA WATCHED in horror as droids swarmed the tank. Luke drove the TIE crawler over the first line of guards, crushing the overseers beneath its heavy treads.

The crawler picked up speed, its armour easily deflecting the droids' blaster fire. Then R2 beeped wildly. He'd spotted another droid running into Luke's path, carrying a small metallic device.

Leia realised what it was and yelled into her comlink: "Luke, one of the guards has a detonator!"

She watched helplessly as the droid threw itself onto

its back, the crawler passing overhead. Leia imagined it
slapping the explosive onto the bottom of the cockpit,
the magnetic seal locking in place, and then . . .

BOOM!

Light blossomed beneath the tank. Leia cried out
as the TIE crawler was thrown into the air. The tank
flipped over and crashed back down, treads buckled
and smoke billowing from its engine.

GO TO PAGE 94.

LUKE'S LIGHTSABER BURST to life with its usual buzz.

"Then fight," he said, dropping into a defensive stance, but that didn't protect him from the rusty pump filter that bounced off the back of his head. He turned around to see the Sullustan lob a power cell at him. The throw was clumsy, but the improvised missile clipped his wrist. Luke dropped his lightsaber, the blade extinguishing as it hit the ground.

"What are you doing?" he spluttered as a power converter struck him on the forehead. He went down hard, slipping on the loose scrap. His vision spun as he heard Leia wrestling with the slaves, who had grabbed her.

He reached for his saber, but a warning shot from one of the approaching droids forced him to raise his hands.

"What happened here?" the droid demanded.

The Sullustan stepped forward. "These offworlders attacked the overseers. It had nothing to do with us."

The human had pinned Leia's arms behind her back. "We captured them for you. It wasn't our fault."

The droid threw two stun collars towards the workers. They landed, binders open, on the ground in front of Luke. "Put those on them."

The Sullustan fastened the collar around Luke's neck.

"Let's see how brave you are now," the grey-skinned alien sneered.

THE END

CAN YOU GO BACK AND HELP LUKE AND LEIA MAKE BETTER CHOICES?

"US?" LUKE WASN'T SURE about this. "Leia, my X-wing is pretty beaten up. . ."

"That's fine," Leia said. "If someone is capturing spacecraft, we need to take something that no one in their right mind would want to steal. A real heap of junk."

"You want to take her *where*?" Han Solo asked, hands on hips. They were standing in *Home One*'s hangar bay in front of the *Millennium Falcon*, Han's pride and joy.

"It's a quick search-and-rescue mission, that's all."

"In the Kiax nebula? What is wrong with you people? I told Mon Mothma that flying through that cloud was a bad idea, but would she listen? It's a dirty place, full of dirty crooks."

Leia shot a glance at Han's battered freighter. "Then the *Falcon* will fit right in."

Han looked at Luke for support. "Did you hear that? She asks for help and then insults my ship."

"C'mon, Han," Luke said. "You'll be doing us a favour."

"Why is it always me that has to do favours?" Han

asked. "Why not ask Syndulla, or even Jaxxon if you're that desperate."

"*No one* is that desperate," Leia said firmly. "Fine. If you don't want to help, you don't have to help."

"I don't want to help," Han confirmed with a tight smile. "Now, if you'll excuse me, I need to help Chewie fix the docking ring."

Luke watched Han swagger towards the large Wookiee, who was busying himself with an arc welder. "Well, I guess the mission's off."

Leia had already started marching towards the turbolift. "Oh, make no mistake – the mission's on!"

"But we don't have a ship," he said, catching up with her.

"Yes, we do," she told him. "We're taking the *Falcon*."

"But Han said—"

"I know what Han said," Leia interrupted as the turbolift doors opened. "But do you *really* think that's going to stop me?"

DOES LUKE HELP LEIA TAKE THE *FALCON*?

YES – GO TO PAGE 40.

NO – TURN TO PAGE 9.

LATER THAT EVENING, Luke and Leia watched R2-D2 lead Han and Chewie from the hangar deck. Luke had thought the smuggler wasn't going to go with the astromech, but he had bought R2's story about being needed on the flight deck.

"Come on," Leia said before disappearing into the *Falcon*.

"Are you sure this is a good idea, Master Luke?" C-3PO asked as they followed her up the ramp.

"No," Luke admitted. "But have you ever tried to say no to her?"

"I wouldn't dream of it. I am programmed to obey without question."

"Then sit over there and be quiet," Luke said as they reached the cockpit.

C-3PO sat down beside the aft bulkhead. "Commencing silence now, sir."

Leia was already in the co-pilot's seat. "We need to hurry."

Luke took Han's seat and activated the ship's repulsors.

Nothing happened.

"Aren't we supposed to be moving?" Leia asked.

Luke checked the fault locators. "I don't understand. Everything's working perfectly."

"If I may, I think I know the problem," C-3PO said. Luke turned to see the droid pointing towards a flashing light on the subspace engine controls. "I believe Captain Solo has installed an immobiliser to prevent his ship from being stolen."

"Who would do such a thing?" Leia commented. "Can you override it?"

"Me? Oh no, Princess. I'm afraid it's far beyond my capabilities. If Artoo were here, I'm sure he could fix the troublesome thing."

"Artoo *is* here," Luke said, sighing.

Leia turned to see an agitated R2-D2 standing in front of the *Falcon* with Han Solo and Chewbacca.

Luke gave them an embarrassed wave. "Are you going to tell him what we're doing, or should I?"

THE END

**CAN YOU GO BACK AND HELP LUKE AND
LEIA MAKE BETTER CHOICES?**

"ARTOO!" LUKE YELLED, igniting his lightsaber.
He was ready to slice the droid from the monster's back
when Leia stopped him.

"Luke, no."

"But Artoo is going to get crushed."

"Look at the crab's eyes, Luke. It's terrified."

Luke did as Leia asked and saw that she was right.
The scrap crab's eyes were wide with fear. It hadn't
attacked them at all. It was making its shell thick to
protect itself.

To protect itself from *them*!

Leia stepped towards the towering beast.

"We don't want to hurt you. Do you understand? We're not a threat."

The crab scuttled back, its claws lowered as if it understood her words. Luke had seen Leia defuse arguments within the Alliance Council and persuade warring planets to join forces to fight the Empire. She was a natural diplomat and a born leader. And now even alien creatures listened to her?

If he didn't know better, Luke would have thought *she* was the one who was supposed to train as a Jedi, not him.

The creature calmed, metal dropping from its shell – including R2-D2, who clattered to the ground with an indignant bloop.

TURN TO PAGE 82.

"HOW ARE WE going to get in?" Leia asked.

"I've got an idea," Luke said. "Wait here."

Before Leia could stop him, Luke ran into the workshop, heading for the large TIE crawler. Dodging guards, Luke jumped onto the back of the tank and dropped into the cockpit.

Once he was inside, Leia's voice burst from his comlink.

"Please tell me you're not planning to drive that thing through a wall."

"I'll draw off the guards," Luke said, settling in behind the controls, "so you and Artoo can sneak in."

"But what if you're caught?"

"They won't stand a chance against this thing," he replied as the crawler jolted forward, lurching towards the tower.

Within seconds, laser bolts were bouncing off the tank's armour as every guard went running towards it.

WHAT DOES LUKE DO?

BLAST THE DROIDS - TURN TO PAGE 86.

CRUSH THE DROIDS - GO TO PAGE 54.

"CONCENTRATE ON the TIE fighters!" Luke yelled.

"Are you sure?"

"Yes. For all we know, they're working together."

She responded by banking hard to port, avoiding a fresh barrage of torpedoes. Luke cleared his mind, trying to block out the sounds of missiles thudding against their shields. He closed his eyes, visualising the TIE fighters, trying to see where they were heading.

An explosion ripped through the *Millennium Falcon*, throwing Luke forward. Smoke was billowing into the gun turret as he yelled into his headset.

"Leia? Are you all right?"

The comm system was down, and he could tell they were drifting.

He scrambled up the ladder towards the cockpit. There was a shot from ahead. A stun beam?

Luke stumbled forward, slamming into a figure in body armour.

"What have we here?" said someone with a guttural voice.

Luke peered through the smoke to see a hulking reptilian with four muscular arms.

"Who are you?"

"The name's Nodo," came the reply. "Where's Solo?"

"Han?' Luke said, reaching for his lightsaber. It was gone. It must have fallen from his belt when they were hit. Luke threw himself at the raider but was held tight by powerful scaled fingers.

"Boss," said someone else behind them – one of Nodo's cronies, Luke supposed, although he couldn't see. His eyes were streaming from the smoke. "Solo isn't on board. There's only a woman."

"Leia!" Luke cried out.

The reptilian grinned. "*Leia Organa?* Well, well . . ."

"Don't hurt her."

The alien increased the pressure on Luke's arms.

"I won't if you tell me where to find Solo."

"You won't be able to get to him," Luke gasped. "He's with the Alliance fleet."

Nodo snorted. "The Rebel Alliance? They recruited a deadbeat like Solo?"

"He's a hero."

"He's no-good scum, that's what he is."

That was why Han hadn't wanted them to take the

ship. He had too many enemies who would recognise the *Millennium Falcon*.

The alien shoved Luke into the waiting hands of his gang. "Lock him up, and the girl, too."

"What are you going to do, Boss?" the lackey asked.

Nodo chuckled. "Contact the Alliance. See if they're agreeable to a prisoner exchange. Leia Organa and this runt for Solo and his Wookiee." He reached forward and grabbed Luke's chin. "Sounds fair, doesn't it, lad?"

THE END

**CAN YOU GO BACK AND HELP LUKE AND
LEIA MAKE BETTER CHOICES?**

"USE YOUR ELECTRO PROD!" Luke yelled. The droid extended a probe that delivered a charge of pure energy to the monster's metal shell. Electricity flowed over the accumulated junk, and the creature let out a fearsome scream.

"Luke, look out!"

Leia dove, knocking Luke out of the way as a cooler unit whizzed over his head to attach itself to the crab's side. More and more metal was flying towards the crustacean, burying R2 beneath a new layer of junk.

WHAT DO THEY DO?

LUKE ATTACKS THE CREATURE - TURN TO PAGE 134.

LEIA SHOUTS AT LUKE NOT TO ATTACK - GO TO PAGE 62.

LUKE YANKED HIS FATHER'S lightsaber from
his belt and ignited it as the raiders boarded the ship.
Luke charged towards the pirates, deflecting shots fired
by a squid-faced Quarren. Behind him, Leia returned
fire, but it soon became clear they were fighting a losing
battle.

Even with the lightsaber, there were too many
enemies. Luke blocked and parried but was distracted
as a pirate droid stunned Leia.

Dropping his guard, Luke received a stun bolt to his side. His lightsaber clattered to the deck.

How would they get out of this one?

THE END

CAN YOU GO BACK AND HELP LUKE AND LEIA MAKE BETTER CHOICES?

BY THE TIME the *Falcon*'s landing gear was deployed, Luke's neck was stiff and his back ached. They waited until they heard the boarding party stomp down the main ramp before lifting the deck plate and clambering out.

Returning to the cockpit, Luke looked out the windows at an expanse of junked technology stretching as far as he could see. Having grown up on Tatooine, he was used to dunes of sand but had never seen hills of wrecked machinery. There were broken-down droids and dozens of spaceships, some intact but most stripped down to their superstructures. Steelpeckers wheeled in the sky above the vast junkyard while figures toiled amid the rubbish, picking over the scrapped star cruisers.

One particular craft caught Leia's attention.

"There," she said, pointing to a medium transport on the horizon.

"Send a message to the fleet, Artoo," Luke instructed the astromech droid. "Tell them we've found the *Nema*."

R2-D2 tried to do as he was told but soon reported that it was impossible.

"The signal's being blocked," Luke said, checking the comm system. "No transmissions can leave the planet."

"Can we at least take off?" Leia asked, sitting in the co-pilot's chair.

R2 delivered more bad news. "The *Falcon's* been clamped," Luke said, interpreting the droid's bleeps.

"Clamped? How?"

"There's only one way to find out," Luke said, handing Leia his blaster. "You may need this."

They crept down the ramp into the vast junkyard. The air was warm and stank of grease, but there was no sign of the raiders who had taken them there. They'd probably gone off to claim payment from whoever ran the place. It wasn't like the *Falcon* was going anywhere, thanks to the large metal clamp attached to its landing gear. There was no way of taking off without ripping the ship in two.

"Look," said Leia, pointing towards a group working in the heat beside what looked like the metal skeleton of a downed Imperial walker. They were surrounded by imposing robots, each holding electro-whips. They looked like old commando droids from the Clone Wars, their armour painted green and a strange symbol emblazoned on their angular chests.

As Luke watched, one of the scavengers stumbled and fell, only to feel the crack of an electro-whip across his back.

"They're slaves," Leia said, horrified.

DO THEY HELP THE SLAVE WORKERS?

YES - TURN TO PAGE 48.

NO - TURN TO PAGE 88.

"IN HERE," LEIA SAID, propelling Luke through a door.

They were in Han's cabin. The place was surprisingly empty, and the walls were bare except for Han's medal of bravery hanging next to a messy bunk.

Leia waited for R2 to wheel in before shutting the door. Luke listened as footsteps passed the cabin and stopped.

The door hissed open, and Luke's hand went to his lightsaber.

"I wouldn't," warned a Lasat holding a bo-rifle. "Drop it."

The Lasat's rifle was joined by numerous other weapons pointing into Han's tiny cabin. Luke had no choice but to obey.

THE END

WHAT CAN YOU CHANGE SO LUKE
AND LEIA AREN'T CAPTURED?

IN THE RAIDING PARTY'S boarding tube, a tall Lasat with a cybernetic eye watched the escape pod explode.

"What was that?" he asked the Nephran beside him.

The lobster-clawed pirate shrugged. "Looked like an escape pod, Grox."

The Lasat's eyes narrowed. "How are you getting on with that door, Kragan?"

The young Quarren who had been struggling with the docking ring stood back as the airlock finally opened. "We're in."

Grox stomped past the Quarren and stepped onto the ship, bo-rifle ready to fire. Kragan and the Nephran followed, the boarding party rounded off by an assassin droid that looked as though it had seen better days.

"Kragan, you and Mirack see if there are any survivors. PALLAS-Eleven, you're with me."

Grox sniffed the air as Kragan and the Nephran hurried off. "Right, let's see how much this junker is worth."

TURN TO PAGE 53.

"ARE YOU THINKING what I'm thinking?" Luke asked as they ran back towards the *Falcon*.

"If there's only one transmitter . . ." Leia started.

"We break into the Tech Masters' citadel and use it to contact the Alliance," Luke finished.

"We owe it to those people to try," Leia said as they found R2, who was struggling across the uneven ground.

Suddenly, Luke was thrown forward! The ground was shifting beneath him as something pushed up to the surface. It was a giant crab with massive claws! Its shell was made up of twisted sheets of metal, and Luke had to duck as machine parts flew through the air to stick to the crab. It was as if the giant crustacean was magnetic. Even R2 was sucked from the ground with a squeal to slam into the ever-growing shell.

WHAT DOES LUKE DO?

**ATTACK THE CREATURE WITH HIS
LIGHTSABER - GO TO PAGE 134.**
**HAVE R2-D2 SHOCK THE CRAB WITH HIS
ELECTRO PROD - TURN TO PAGE 69.**

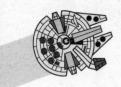

THE *NEMA* WAS ALREADY docked with *Home One* when Luke dropped out of hyperspace.

He activated the comlink. "Leia?"

"Ready to face the music?" she replied.

"No," he admitted, swinging the *Falcon* into *Home One*'s hangar bay.

Han Solo was waiting for Luke as he walked down the ramp.

"If you've so much as put a dent in her . . ." the former smuggler began.

"You'll barely notice the difference," Leia said, joining them beside the ship.

"Oh, no, you don't," Han said, turning on the princess. "You steal my ship, you lose the right to bad-mouth her."

"We brought her back, didn't we?" Luke said. "And the medical transport, too."

"That's not the point," Han snapped. "There are people out there who would love to get their hands on the *Falcon*. Bad people . . . *dangerous* people. Anything could have happened to you."

"We get it," Leia said, raising her hands. "We shouldn't have taken the *Falcon*."

"Leia's right," Luke agreed. "We know what she means to you."

"What *she* means to me?" Han repeated, looking at Luke as if he was crazy. "Listen, kid, the *Falcon's* the best there is, but she's just a ship. Ships can be replaced. But you two . . . you're . . ."

He caught Leia's eye and trailed off. "Well . . . just don't do it again."

"Careful, hotshot," Leia said, smiling at the smuggler. "You almost sound like you care."

Han tried to look innocent. "Me? Care about you? I'm just glad you came back so I can watch Mon Mothma throw you both in the brig."

"She's not happy, huh?" Luke said, rubbing the back of his neck.

"Not in the slightest, and I can't say I blame her. Of all the dumb stunts to pull . . ." And with that, Han's face broke into a grin. "Couldn't have done better myself."

THE END

**CONGRATULATIONS! YOU'VE REACHED
THE END OF THE ADVENTURE.**

"LUKE, WE DON'T HAVE time," Leia insisted.
"We owe Artoo so much, but we can't risk everything
just to save him."

Luke nodded sadly. "You're right, but—"

"But it doesn't make it any easier," Leia said,
squeezing his arm. "Come on. We need to decide what
to do."

WHAT DO THEY DO?

SHUT DOWN THE SHIELD - TURN TO PAGE 104.

CONTACT THE ALLIANCE - GO TO PAGE 129.

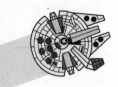

R2 STRUGGLED OVER TO Luke as the gigantic crab retreated back under the debris.

"That was incredible," Luke told Leia, but she just wiped metal filings from her sleeve.

"Perhaps I should have asked it to give us a lift to the city." She glanced at the towers in the distance. "It's going to be a long walk."

"Unless we use this," Luke said, finding a long metal board in the junk. Stepping on it, he jabbed a control with his toe and the board rose unsteadily from the ground.

Leia didn't look convinced. "A skimboard? Do you even know how to fly it?"

"I can fly anything."

"Now you sound like Han."

"Thanks."

"It wasn't a compliment," she told him, finally clambering on with R2.

Luke was a better skim surfer than Leia had given him credit for. He only tipped them over three, maybe four times before they reached the edge of the city.

It didn't take long to find the Tech Masters' citadel.

It was the tallest and most imposing building in the city on the edge of the junk wastes, and it cast a long shadow across the factories and work camps that refined all the salvaged scrap. There was a strange-looking tank that seemed to be constructed from a TIE fighter, with massive crawler treads instead of wings. Components and machine parts were piled high, and slave workers hauled hoversleds under the watchful eyes of overseer droids.

HOW DO THEY GET INTO THE CITADEL?

BY USING FORCE - TURN TO PAGE 65.
BY USING STEALTH - GO TO PAGE 92.

"WHY DON'T YOU FIGHT BACK?" Luke asked.

"What's the point?" the human asked. "There are too many droids."

The Sullustan agreed. "Strike one down and the Tech Masters send three in its place."

WHAT DO THEY SAY TO THE SLAVES?

"WHO ARE THE TECH MASTERS?" - TURN TO PAGE 106.

"YOU SHOULDN'T BE SO COWARDLY!" - GO TO PAGE 90.

"WE UNDERSTAND," Leia told them, "but we can't give up. My friend destroyed an entire battle station, the same battle station that annihilated my homeworld. We know what it's like to face overwhelming odds, but we also know that you can still succeed."

The human took a step forward. "Are you talking about the Death Star? That was you?"

Luke smiled proudly. "It was, although I wasn't exactly on my own. I was helped by my friends."

A high-pitched hum reached them across the wastes. Luke turned to see speeder bikes racing towards them.

"Overseer droids," the human explained. "You should go. Both of you. We'll cover for you."

"We will?" the Sullustan asked.

The Rodian nodded. "Yes. If what they say is true, then perhaps they really can get off this greaseball."

"We'll take you, too," Leia promised. "If we can take down that force field."

"Then go," the human said, picking up a blaster, "before we change our minds."

TURN TO PAGE 77.

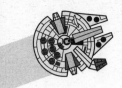

THE POD SHUDDERED as its blaster cannons discharged. The beams tore through the first line of droids, but the mechanical guards kept coming, more than Luke could ever hope to hit.

Luke reversed, blinded by blaster fire. Shots rang off the tank's armour plating as cracks snaked across the viewport.

Leia watched in horror as the droids delivered a devastating strike to the crawler's caterpillar tracks. The tread jammed, the tank shuddering to a halt.

Drawing her blaster, she ran to Luke's aid, firing wildly. Jumping onto the crawler, Leia flung open the hatch to find Luke unconscious. A stun blast had struck him through the shattered viewport.

She tried to haul him out of the pod, but she already knew there was no escape. Commando droids were advancing on their position from all directions, blasters and vibroswords raised. What could they do now?

THE END

**CAN YOU GO BACK AND HELP LUKE AND
LEIA MAKE BETTER CHOICES?**

LEIA DREW HER BLASTER. "We need to help them."

Luke hesitated. "No. There are too many droids. We wouldn't stand a chance."

"We have to at least try."

By the walker, the droid with the electro-whip looked up.

"It sees us!" Leia shouted, dropping to one knee and opening fire.

The droids whirled around, blasters blazing. Luke was forced to drop back, blocking shot after shot with his lightsaber. A shot ricocheted off the *Falcon's* hull, clipping his shoulder. He tumbled forward, stunned but not unconscious. The lightsaber slipped from his hand, coming to rest beneath the foot of one of the advancing droids.

He looked up to see Leia slump to the ground, knocked back by a stun beam. Above them, the droid with the electro-whip ordered the slaves to fetch shock collars.

"Inform the Tech Masters we have two more workers," it buzzed. Luke could barely move as the collar was snapped around his neck and he was dragged to his feet.

"We'll escape," he promised the droid, his voice weak.

"Escape is impossible. From this day on you will serve the Tech Masters. You can start by stripping this cruiser of all essential systems."

Luke realised the droid was talking about the *Falcon*. "Although by the look of it, that won't take long!"

THE END

CAN YOU GO BACK AND HELP LUKE AND LEIA MAKE BETTER CHOICES?

"YOU SHOULDN'T BE so cowardly," Luke said, instantly regretting his words.

"Cowardly?" cried the human. "You have no idea what it's like, working out here in the heat all day, with barely any food or rest. . ."

The slave glanced over Luke's shoulder as a whine filled the air. Luke turned to see commando droids rushing towards them on speeder bikes.

"What did we tell you?" the Sullustan snarled. "They'll make us suffer for this."

TURN TO PAGE 56.

"LUKE, WE'LL NEVER find him in time."

Behind them Everson groaned, coming around. Luke hurried over and crouched in front of the dazed man.

"Where do they take droids for processing?" he asked.

The man's eyes rolled in their sockets. Luke didn't need to use the Force. Everson was so disoriented he would have answered anything.

"Two levels up," he slurred. "The dismantling suites."

"I don't like the sound of that," Luke said, jumping back up.

TURN TO PAGE 126.

LUKE REACHED for his lightsaber.

"No," Leia said. "We can't fight our way in."

"Then how are we going to get into the citadel?"

Leia found a circular hatch bolted into the middle of the road. "Artoo, can you cut through this?"

The droid quickly produced a fusion torch. Soon R2 had uncovered an awaiting repulsor platform below.

Luke put a hand across his nose. "Ugh!"

Leia jumped down onto the platform. "Sewer pipes. Even palaces have them. Come on."

Luke ignited his lightsaber, illuminating slimy walls as they trudged towards the citadel. He didn't want to think about what was in the water. The sewer smelled worse than an eopie stable.

"Do you think we've gone far enough?" he asked as they reached another repulsor platform.

"Maybe," Leia replied, "although if we go farther we'll definitely be under the tower."

WHAT SHOULD THEY DO?

CONTINUE ALONG THE TUNNEL - GO TO PAGE 105.

USE THE PLATFORM - TURN TO PAGE 114.

"COULDN'T YOU HAVE fought back?" Luke asked.

"Do you see this?" the human said, pulling up his tunic to reveal a puckered scar. "I fought back once. Even took out an overseer. Three more droids were sent in its place."

"A punishment squad," said Leia.

He nodded. "They did this. And worse."

WHAT DOES LUKE SAY TO HIM?

"THERE ARE ENOUGH SHIPS HERE. WHY DON'T YOU ESCAPE?" - TURN TO PAGE 51.

"YOU SHOULDN'T GIVE UP SO EASILY" - GO TO PAGE 101.

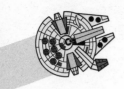

LUKE WOKE TO FIND himself being dragged into a grand chamber by two overseer droids. He could see through the large windows that they were up high, almost at the top of the Tech Masters' citadel, but Luke had no idea how he had gotten there. The last thing he remembered was thundering the crawler towards the wall, followed by a flash of intense light and heat.

A human walked ahead of the droids, luxurious robes sweeping across a marble floor. They stopped in front of a raised platform where three figures sat on large hovering thrones. A Dyplotid sat in the center with a Keredian, complete with cyberoptic implant, to the right and a bulky Elnacon to the left.

"What have we here, Everson?" the Dyplotid asked.

"The prisoner attempted to steal a century tank, Lord Craykan," the human replied in a surprisingly shrill voice.

"Why bring him to us?" the Elnacon asked, glaring at Luke through her protective face globe.

"He was carrying this, Lady Yarla." Everson held Luke's lightsaber for the Tech Masters to see.

All four of Craykan's eyes widened. "A Jedi?"

"Don't be ridiculous," the Keredian snapped. "The Jedi are extinct."

"Yes, Lord Ruk," Everson said. "But think of what you could learn from such a weapon."

Craykan fixed his gaze on Luke. "What do you want of us?"

"We want our ships," he replied.

"They are ours now," Yarla told him. "Everything on this planet belongs to us."

"But you don't understand. Your pirates stole a medical transport. We need those supplies."

"Is this true?" Craykan asked Everson. The human

produced a sleek dataslate from the sleeve of his robe and checked the screen.

"Three ships have recently been delivered by our associates. The first two have been stripped of their assets, but the third has yet to be unloaded."

"And the crews?"

Everson scrolled down his report. "They resisted and were executed."

"A pity," the Dyplotid commented.

"A pity?" Luke spat. "They were members of the Rebellion. They were fighting for freedom."

"Rebellion?" Ruk asked, looking confused. "What Rebellion?"

Luke frowned. "Against the Empire, of course."

"Ah, I see," the Keredian said, waving a dismissive hand. "The Galactic War is no concern of ours."

"No concern? *Millions* die at the Emperor's hands every day."

"So?" Yarla cut in. "Trionak is safe. That is all that matters."

WHAT DOES LUKE DO?

ATTACK THEM - TURN TO PAGE 136.
REASON WITH THEM - GO TO PAGE 120.

"ONLY IF YOU'RE SURE," Luke told the droid, who hurried over to the clamps.

Luke watched as Leia ushered slaves on board the *Nema* and took off. It was Luke and R2's turn to escape.

"What's taking so long, Artoo?" The droid honked, admitting defeat. "What do you mean you can't do it?"

Suddenly, a familiar howl filled the air. An Imperial TIE fighter was hovering in front of them.

"Surrender immediately," the pilot ordered over the fighter's loudspeakers.

Luke activated his lightsaber.

"You have to make me first."

The TIE pilot fired without hesitation. Luke tried to deflect the bolt of emerald energy, but it was too powerful. He was thrown back against the *Millennium Falcon*, his lightsaber flying from his hand.

Luke and R2 were in trouble, but Leia would come back for them . . . wouldn't she?

THE END

CAN YOU GO BACK AND HELP LUKE AND
LEIA MAKE BETTER CHOICES?

LUKE'S HAND WENT to the lightsaber that hung from his belt.

"No," Leia said, leaping up to stop him. "We don't know how many there are."

"What do you want us to do? Surrender?"

"We use our heads. The *Falcon* has escape pods, right?"

"You want us to abandon ship?"

"Not exactly."

Luke led Leia and R2 through the darkened ship as the raiders attempted to open the cruiser's temperamental airlock.

"Here they are," he said as they reached the escape pods.

Leia turned to their droid. "Artoo, tell me these things have independent power sources."

The astromech honked that she was correct.

"Great." Leia pulled her blaster from its holster on her waist and twisted a control on the pistol's grip.

"What are you doing?" Luke asked as the weapon started to whine.

"Overloading the power pack," she replied, opening the nearest pod.

"But it'll explode."

"Exactly." Leia threw the blaster into the pod and slammed the door shut. "If we eject the pod and it explodes in space . . ."

"The pirates will think we blew ourselves up trying to escape!" Luke said.

Leia rewarded him with a smile. "This is a smuggler's ship. There must be all kinds of nooks and crannies. We find a hiding place and get a message back to the fleet."

She pulled down the launch handle.

Nothing happened.

She tried again.

"I don't believe it! Not even his escape pods work!"

The pistol's whine was reaching a crescendo.

Luke tried the controls. "The locking mechanism's rusted."

"So instead of blowing up the pod, we're going to blow up the *Falcon!*"

Luke tried the door. "Not if we power down the blaster."

"Let me guess . . ." Leia said as he slapped the glass in frustration.

"Locked tight."

"Perhaps facing the pirates wasn't such a bad idea," Leia admitted.

"I can do this," Luke said, raising an open palm towards the escape pod. He reached out with the Force, trying to manipulate the lock. When that didn't work, he put pressure on the escape pod itself, but try as he might, the pod wouldn't budge. It was like trying to push his hand through solid rock.

He couldn't give up. Gritting his teeth, he tried again, pushing so hard he thought his head might burst...

And the pod shot into space.

"I did it!" Luke exclaimed, laughing with delight. "I really did it."

Then his gaze dropped to R2, who had his probe connected to an access port. Luke's shoulders slumped. "No. *You* did it, didn't you?"

The droid bleeped happily at his master.

"You can feel sorry for yourself later," Leia told him. "That docking ring won't hold them for long."

TURN TO PAGE 76.

"YOU SHOULDN'T GIVE UP so easily," Luke said.

"Shouldn't give up?" the Rodian repeated. "Do you know what happened the last time there was a revolt?"

Luke shook his head. "No, I—"

The green-scaled alien didn't give him a chance to finish. "The Tech Masters took away our rations for a week. We were forced to survive on whatever bugs we could find among the scrap metal."

Leia stepped in, ever the diplomat. "We're sorry. We didn't know."

"No," said the Sullustan. "You were too busy telling us what we should have done."

The sound of speeder bikes made them all turn. Armed droids were sweeping across the junk wastes.

"What did we tell you?" the Sullustan snarled. "They'll make us suffer for this."

TURN TO PAGE 56.

"NO," LUKE SAID. "You couldn't do it before."

Then he heard a clacking noise behind him. Luke turned to see not one but three scrap crabs rising to the surface, metal flying through the air towards their magnetic shells.

"Artoo, get up the ramp," he said as the *Falcon* lurched towards the panicked crabs. The clamps creaked against the strain of holding the ship in place while Luke helped the astromech up the boarding ramp and raced to the cockpit.

Outside, the crabs were all but cocooned in metal to protect them from the battle. With the sound of ripping metal, the clamps broke and the *Falcon* was free, skidding towards the trio of terrified crustaceans.

Luke yanked back on the flight stick, hoping the *Falcon*'s engines were stronger than the magnetic pull of the creatures. The ship shuddered and then rocketed into the sky. Luke glanced down at the ground to check that the crabs were okay, but the crustaceans had already burrowed back beneath the metal dunes.

"Leia?" he called into his headset as he weaved among warring starfighters. "Are you there?"

R2 bleeped as the *Nema* streaked past them, heading for the stars.

"Just try to keep up," Leia said as the two ships cleared orbit. *"Last one back to the fleet faces Mon Mothma!"*

Luke watched the *Nema* swing around Admiral Rhodes's Star Destroyer before escaping into hyperspace.

It wasn't Mon Mothma he was worried about.

TURN TO PAGE 78.

LUKE HURRIED BACK TO EVERSON.

"Where do you control the planetary shield?"

The man groaned but didn't answer.

Luke tried again. "You will tell me where to shut down the planetary shield."

"L-level two," the man slurred, his eyes rolling. "Can't miss it."

TURN TO PAGE 132.

THEY CONTINUED, but it soon became clear that there were no more platforms.

"You were right," Leia finally admitted, the stink growing unbearable. "We should go back."

Something splashed in the water behind them.

"Back isn't an option," Luke said, running farther into the sewer pipe only to slide to a halt when the glow of his saber illuminated a pair of gigantic claws.

A scrap crab blocked their path, a flashing cybernetic implant fixed between its frenzied eyestalks.

"I thought these things were timid!" Luke yelled as another scuttled up behind them.

"They've been turned into guard dogs," Leia said, drawing her blaster. "I guess trying to sneak in wasn't such a great idea."

Luke and Leia stood back to back as the giant crabs attacked, pincers clacking wildly.

THE END

**CAN YOU GO BACK AND HELP LUKE AND
LEIA MAKE BETTER CHOICES?**

"WHO ARE THE TECH MASTERS?" Leia asked.

"You'll find out soon enough," someone said.

A hunched Rodian stepped out from behind the human. She was as malnourished as the other slaves and was missing one of her saucer-like antennae.

"What does that mean?" Luke asked, who knew a little Rodian from growing up on Tatooine.

"They rule this place," the alien replied.

"A junkyard?" Leia asked.

The Rodian snorted. "The Tech Masters live there" – she pointed towards a city, its towers gleaming on the horizon – "in the citadel."

"And that's who hijacked our ship?"

The Sullustan laughed. "Like they would do anything for themselves. The Masters live in luxury. They hire privateers to capture ships and cargo, dumping them here for us to salvage."

Leia looked at the mountains of scrap. "Why?"

"To strip them of anything the Masters want," the human said. "Anything that can make their lives more . . . *comfortable*."

"And what if the ships still have crews?"

"How do you think *we* got here?" the Rodian replied.

WHAT DOES LUKE SAY TO THEM?

**"COULDN'T YOU HAVE FOUGHT
BACK?" - TURN TO PAGE 93.**
**"THERE ARE ENOUGH SHIPS HERE. WHY
DON'T YOU ESCAPE?" - GO TO PAGE 51.**

"THERE'S NO GUARANTEE that we'll even be able to get a message through to the Alliance," Luke told Leia. "We have to take out the shield."

"In the Tech Masters' throne room," Leia reminded him.

"I never said it would be easy."

Leia drew her blaster. "That hasn't stopped us before."

But the throne room was empty when they crept out of the turbolift. Luke discovered a holotable hidden behind the tapestries on the back wall.

"That must be the shield," Leia said, pointing towards the flickering image of Trionak cocooned in a transparent bubble. "Can you deactivate it?"

"No," Luke admitted. "But Artoo can."

The little droid trundled around the table and found an access point. He went to work, bleeping happily before squealing as electricity surged along his probe. With a final squawk, the droid toppled onto his back and lay still.

"Artoo!" Luke cried, vaulting over the table. The astromech was on his back, smoke curling from sparking servomotors.

"What happened?" Leia asked.

Luke tried to reactivate the droid. "I don't know. He must have triggered something. His circuits are fried."

"Did you really think we would leave our systems unprotected?" Craykan said as he stepped through the curtains, flanked by a squadron of commando droids. "Anyone attempting to deactivate the planetary shield without the correct authorisation automatically triggers a failsafe."

"You mean a booby trap," Luke said.

Craykan smiled. "Don't worry, we'll put your little friend to good use. Now . . . drop your weapons."

Luke and Leia had no choice but to obey.

"That's better. You really made a nuisance of yourselves, overcoming poor Everson like that. We were forced to throw him to the scrap crabs as punishment."

"You're monsters!" Leia spat.

"No - *they* are, as you'll find out soon enough." Craykan turned to his guards. "Take them to the pit. The scrap crabs won't believe their luck."

THE END

CAN YOU GO BACK AND HELP LUKE AND LEIA MAKE BETTER CHOICES?

"READY . . ." THE DROID INTONED, "aim . . ."

A streak of blue energy slashed through the robot before it could complete its order. It collapsed to the floor, revealing a familiar figure brandishing Luke's lightsaber.

"Leia?" Luke asked in amazement.

She didn't have time to answer, swivelling to slice through the next droid's blaster, a strike delivered more by luck than with judgment. The droid reacted, catching Leia with the back of its hand. She stumbled towards Luke, his saber whirling through the air.

Luke threw his hands up to protect himself, and the blade sliced through the energy cuffs. He pushed out with the Force, knocking the droid into the remaining two guards. As the robots clattered together, Leia pressed his father's weapon into Luke's hands.

"Perhaps I'll stick with this," she said, drawing her blaster to deliver two crisp shots into the tangle of robots. The bolts hit a droid between the photoreceptors, its head exploding.

"Not bad," Luke commented before the droid Leia had disarmed jumped forward, vibrosword buzzing

in hand. Luke blocked the whirring blade, the two combatants straining against each other. Luke trusted in the Force, letting it tell him when to feint to the side so the droid tumbled forward, betrayed by its own momentum. Another slash of the saber and it was split in two.

Luke looked up, ready to lunge at the last guard, but the droid was already on the floor, smoke curling from its servos. Leia lowered her weapon and turned to him.

"You know, we make a pretty good team."

"Where did you come from?" he asked, extinguishing his saber.

"Who do you think was under the hood?" she said with a smile. The servant at the turbolift – that had been Leia!

"But how did you know we were coming down?"

She shrugged. "I don't know. A feeling I guess."

"And Artoo?"

Her smile dropped away. "I lost him."

"What?"

"Your plan worked," she admitted, "more or less. The guards ran to stop you, and we slipped in. Unfortunately, there were more guards inside. I got away, but Artoo ..."

"Artoo got captured."

She nodded.

"We need to find him," Luke said, slipping his saber into his belt.

Leia shook her head. "We don't have time. We need to bring down the planetary shield, or at least try to contact the Alliance."

"We will," Luke promised her. "After we've rescued Artoo."

DOES LEIA AGREE TO RESCUE R2?

YES - TURN TO PAGE 91.

NO - GO TO PAGE 81.

"NO, WE SHOULD DEFINITELY GO UP," Luke told her, jumping onto the platform. "Up is good."

He helped Leia lift R2 and pressed the control.

"It's locked," Leia said as they reached the hatch.

Luke used his lightsaber to cut out the metal disc, then he used R2 to climb out of the hole he'd created.

"What are you waiting for?" Leia hissed as Luke froze, balancing on the droid's dome.

Suddenly, mechanical hands grabbed Luke and pulled him through the hatch. A human appeared above Leia, surrounded by armed guards.

"Did you honestly think we wouldn't notice someone cutting through an access hatch?" His eyes narrowed as he stared at Leia. "You look familiar."

"I'm no one," she said, her hand on her blaster.

"Then you won't mind surrendering," the man sneered.

WHAT DOES LEIA DO?

SURRENDER - TURN TO PAGE 125.

TRY TO ESCAPE - GO TO PAGE 133.

"I SEE THAT YOU survived our firing squad," Craykan said as the pirates delivered Luke, Leia, and R2 to the Tech Masters.

"We found them making a nuisance of themselves in the droid bays," Grox said, Luke's lightsaber in his hand. "Pretty weapons, too. Worth a few credits if you ask me."

"You have been paid enough," Craykan told the Lasat.

A sneer spread across Grox's face. "Is that right? Perhaps I should send them back to the transmitter they were using."

Yarla sat forward in her chair. "Transmitter? Who were you contacting, human?"

Luke gave her as confident a smile as he could muster. "You'll find out soon enough."

"What does that mean?" Ruk bellowed.

"It means this is your last chance to join us," Luke told the Keredian.

"Against the Empire?" Craykan said. "We've told you . . . we have no interest in joining your war."

"Because you wish to hide away from the galaxy."

"Correct."

Beside Luke, Leia smiled. "I have a feeling the galaxy is about to come knocking. . ."

An alarm blared in the corridor outside. Everson ran into the chamber, his face flushed. "Your Graces, an Imperial Star Destroyer has dropped out of hyperspace above Trionak."

"What?" Craykan snapped.

"It's firing on the planetary shield."

Grox's wristlink bleeped. "A transmission is coming in on all frequencies," he reported, activating the link. A voice boomed out of the device.

"This is Admiral Rhodes of the Galactic Empire. You will surrender immediately or face the consequences of your actions."

"The shield will protect us," Ruk insisted, just before the sound of an explosion rumbled through the citadel.

"That may have been true of Alliance ships," Leia told the Keredian as the ground shook, "but not a Star Destroyer. Admiral Rhodes has enough firepower to reduce your paradise to ashes."

"Evacuate the city!" Craykan cried, hitting a control on his sleeve. All three thrones shot up, disappearing through a hatch in the ceiling.

"Cowards!" Grox bellowed at his fleeing employers

before turning to run himself. "Come on, lads. I'm not waiting around to get into a scrap with the Empire."

The pirates ran for the turbolift as the tower was bombarded from space. A large crack appeared and the ceiling to the lift chamber collapsed, burying Grox and his crew. Luke turned at a familiar sound. TIE fighters were screeching past the cracked windows. *Imperial* TIE fighters.

"Looks like Admiral Rhodes has lowered the shield for us," Leia said. "Want to get back to the *Falcon*?"

Luke turned to the pile of rubble that had buried Grox and held out his hand. There was a scrape of metal against marble, and Luke's lightsaber flew from the debris. He caught it midair.

"I thought you'd never ask."

Outside, the city was in chaos, bolts of energy streaming from above. TIE fighters battled TIE fighters in the sky, the Tech Masters' stolen fleet coming up against the real deal.

On the ground, Luke looked around, suddenly realising that he and R2 had lost Leia as they ran from the citadel. "Artoo? Where's the princess? Where's Leia?"

The droid bleeped as Leia of Alderaan zoomed through the chaos on the back of the skimboard. She swept to a halt in front of the dumbstruck Jedi in training and held out her hand.

"Well, what are you waiting for? Get on!"

Luke had to admit that Leia knew what she was doing. The skimboard zipped across the junk wastes, narrowly avoiding a TIE fighter that crashed to the ground in front of them.

Before long, she had gotten them back to the *Millennium Falcon*, still clamped where they'd left it.

"You take the *Falcon*," Leia told Luke as he helped R2 from the board. "I'll round up as many workers as I can. We'll follow you in the *Nema*."

"Are you sure?" Luke asked, but Leia was already rocketing across the scrap dunes, shouting for the slaves to follow her.

Luke was about to run up the ramp into the *Falcon* when he remembered the clamps on its landing gear.

"How are we going to get these off?" he asked R2, who bleeped that he could try to release them.

SHOULD LUKE LET R2 TRY?

YES - TURN TO PAGE 97.

NO - TURN TO PAGE 102.

"YOU CAN'T MEAN THAT," Luke said.

"I assure you I do," the Elnacon replied. "We have created a paradise."

"Built on slavery. And stolen technology."

"On *improved* technology," Yarla insisted, the feathers of her cloak rustling. "Technology that keeps us safe from outsiders like you."

"The same outsiders you plunder and execute!" Luke exclaimed. He decided to try a different tactic. If Leia was there, she would try to reason with her captors. He was no diplomat – and the thought of making deals with such murderers made his stomach churn – but he was willing to try anything. "You're right, you *have* created a paradise, but think what difference you could make if you joined us."

Ruk snorted. "Joined you?"

"Against the Empire. I've seen your starfighters. They're impressive."

"Thank you." The Keredian smirked, displaying a row of golden teeth. "They're a particular passion of mine."

"Then make that passion count. The Alliance desperately needs ships." Another thought struck him. "And a new base."

Craykan frowned. "And you want to come here? To Trionak."

"It's perfect," Luke said. "The Empire would never find us in the nebula."

"Exactly," Yarla cut in. "We have kept this planet secret for centuries. No one must know of our existence."

"But—"

"But nothing," Craykan said. "We have heard enough. You attack us and then ask for our help."

"You attacked us first," Luke retorted.

"And now we will finish it. Everson, dispose of this troublemaker at once."

WHAT DOES LUKE DO?

ATTACK THE TECH MASTERS - GO TO PAGE 136.

ALLOW HIMSELF TO BE LED AWAY - TURN TO PAGE 130.

"LET'S CONTACT THE FLEET," Luke started, "unless..."

Leia narrowed her eyes. "Luke?"

Luke didn't stop to explain his plan, knowing full well that she would try to stop him. Instead, he turned to the droid.

"Artoo, can you open a channel to the nearest Imperial base?"

"The nearest *what*?"

"Trust me," Luke said as a tinny voice came over the speakers.

"This is Imperial listening post two-two-zero-eight."

"I hope you know what you're doing!" Leia hissed.

So do I, Luke thought.

"Listening post," he said into the terminal's comlink, "I am broadcasting from Trionak, a planet in the Kiax nebula. We have discovered a cache of stolen Imperial technology."

"I find that hard to believe," the Imperial officer said.

"I have proof – the memory banks of a probe droid."

Leia shot out a hand to mute the conversation. "What are you *doing*? That data will be invaluable."

"Unless we can get off this planet, the data's pretty useless," he told her, then reactivated the signal.

"Hello?" the officer was saying. *"Are you there?"*

"Sorry. We got cut off," Luke said. "Interference from the nebula. We will now broadcast data from the probe as proof that the Tech Masters have been stealing Imperial data."

"The Tech Masters? Who are the Tech Masters?"

"Enemies of the Empire," he replied. "Transmitting now."

He nodded at R2, who started the transmission, Leia's precious intel streaming across space.

"This is . . . incredible," the Imperial stammered when she'd had a chance to review the message. *"That data is highly classified."*

"Not anymore," Luke said. "And you should see what else the Tech Masters have stolen. TIE fighters, walkers . . . the works."

"You will transmit the coordinates of this planet," the officer commanded.

"Right away," Luke agreed, nodding at R2. "There. Do you have them?"

There was nothing but silence. "Hello?"

Behind them, a boot scraped on the floor. Luke and Leia turned to see the pirate crew who had captured the *Falcon*. They had their blasters drawn and pointing straight at the rebels.

"Talking to someone?" Grox sneered.

TURN TO PAGE 115.

LEIA HAD NO CHOICE but to surrender. She and Luke were marched through the citadel, R2 having been taken away by the armed droids.

The next day she was back out in the junk wastes, a collar around her neck and an overseer droid keeping an electronic eye on her and her fellow slaves. She had no idea where Luke had been taken. They had been assigned to different work parties, and for all she knew they were kilometres apart. But wherever he was, Leia knew he'd be thinking the same thing.

They'd find a way to escape somehow. They had to. . .

THE END

CAN YOU GO BACK AND HELP LUKE AND

LEIA MAKE BETTER CHOICES?

THEY MADE IT BACK to the turbolift without being discovered and ascended to the dismantling suites. The entire level was separated into numerous noisy workshops, droids of all shapes and sizes being picked apart by machines with telescopic arms.

Luke and Leia crept from room to room, keeping their heads down until they found R2 suspended in a dismantler. The Nephran from the boarding party was at the controls, pressing buttons with the tip of his fearsome claw.

"Stop," Luke commanded, stepping up behind the alien. "You don't want to hurt that droid."

"Eh?" the Nephran privateer said, whirling around, but before Luke could try another mind trick, a well-aimed stun bolt knocked the operator to the ground.

"Don't look so disappointed," said Leia as she holstered her blaster. "Besides, that's what you get for hijacking the *Falcon*."

"Now who sounds like Han?"

"Be quiet and help," she said, attempting to free R2 from his restraints.

Luke helped her lower him to the floor, and the droid bleeped his gratitude.

"Don't mention it," Luke said, checking R2's systems as Leia glanced around the room. The place was littered with robots in various stages of dismemberment.

"Is that an Imperial probe?" she asked, finding a cylindrical droid with multiple manipulator arms. "Artoo, can you download its memory?"

"Do we have time?" Luke asked as R2 went to work.

"Just think what we could do with all that data."

R2 whistled that the memory extraction was complete.

"Artoo, can you find the location of the shield controller?" Luke asked.

The droid trundled over to a computer terminal and activated a holographic plan of the building.

"Oh, great," Luke said, pointing towards the top of the tower. "It's in the Tech Masters' main chamber, behind their thrones."

"What about the transmitter?"

R2 booped happily.

"He says he can access it from here," Luke said.

WHAT SHOULD THEY DO NEXT?

SHUT DOWN THE PLANETARY SHIELD - GO TO PAGE 108.

CONTACT THE ALLIANCE - TURN TO PAGE 122.

"WE NEED TO CONTACT the Alliance," Luke said.

"Agreed," Leia said, leading him towards a comm station. Luke tried to open a channel but hit a problem.

"The transmitter's encoded," he told her. "There's no way to access it, not without Artoo."

"Okay," she said, trying to keep Luke calm. "How do we find him?"

Luke was already checking records. "He's being held two levels up . . . in the dismantling suites!"

TURN TO PAGE 126.

THERE WAS NOTHING Luke could do, not with his hands still bound and his saber in Everson's gloved hand. A blaster jabbed into his back, and he was marched into a turbolift. He didn't fight back, not yet. He had to buy himself time . . . and retrieve his lightsaber.

If he tried to snatch his father's weapon using the Force, Everson would just order the droids to fire, but there was another option, a Jedi talent Luke had seen Ben use on Tatooine.

The turbolift doors opened, depositing them in a grimy prison block. A hooded servant was waiting for them, alongside two more droids. Everson handed the woman Luke's lightsaber, instructing her to perform a full scan of the weapon. The servant nodded, hurrying away as Luke was shoved into a small room.

"Back against the wall," Everson ordered Luke as the four droids formed a firing squad.

Luke did what he was told, trying to focus on the human rather than the blasters.

"You don't want to do this," Luke said, willing Everson to obey his words.

A look of doubt flickered over the man's face. "What?"

"You want to let me go."

Everson's eyes seemed to lose focus. "I want to let you go," he repeated dumbly.

Luke's pulse quickened. It was working.

"The droids will lower their weapons," he said calmly.

Everson turned towards the firing squad. "Lower your weapons."

But the droids didn't move.

"Didn't you hear him?" Luke asked them.

"You are to be executed by order of the Tech Masters," one of the droids replied.

Luke's mouth went dry. "No. You will let me go."

"We will let him go," Everson echoed.

"Prepare to fire," the droid snapped, ignoring his human superior.

"Stop them!" Luke shouted. Unable to resist, Everson jumped forward but was swatted away by a droid. He crashed against the wall and slid to the floor, stunned.

Luke didn't know what to do. He was cornered and facing an enemy immune to Jedi mind tricks. There was no way to escape.

TURN TO PAGE 110.

THEY FOUND A TURBOLIFT and headed to
level two. Luke couldn't believe how easy it had been to
influence Everson's mind.

"So," Leia said, "we sabotage the shield and get back
to the *Falcon* – agreed?"

Luke nodded. "Agreed."

The turbolift doors opened and he gasped.

They had been deposited not at the shield control
level but at the battle droids' barracks. As one, every
head snapped towards them and Leia leapt for the
turbolift controls.

She never made it. A hail of stun bolts slammed into
the lift, stopping her in her tracks. Luke activated his
saber, but there were too many of them. As a stun bolt
pinned him against the wall, he realised what a fool he
had been. He hadn't clouded Everson's mind at all. The
man had sent them into a trap.

THE END

**CAN YOU GO BACK AND HELP LUKE AND
LEIA MAKE BETTER CHOICES?**

LEIA DREW HER BLASTER and fired, stunning the human. The droids responded by unloading a volley of plasma bolts into the hole. The energy blasts slammed into R2, sending him flying.

Leia had no option but to jump, landing awkwardly in the murky water at the bottom of the pipe. Her knee twisted beneath her, and she threw out her hands to stop herself from falling flat on her face.

She'd dropped her blaster. Ignoring the pain in her leg, she groped in the darkness as the platform descended, loaded with armed guards.

This time there was no way to escape.

THE END

CAN YOU GO BACK AND HELP LUKE AND

LEIA MAKE BETTER CHOICES?

LUKE LEAPT FORWARD, igniting his father's lightsaber. The blade sang through the air, slicing deep into the crab's scavenged shell. The creature roared in fury and swiped at Luke with a metal-encrusted claw.

"Luke!" Leia cried as Luke went flying. He hit the ground hard, his lightsaber bouncing away.

Leia ran to where he lay, turning him over as the scrap crab burrowed back into the mound of twisted metal, taking R2 with it. Luke was barely conscious and had a deep cut on his forehead.

He groaned as Leia tried to make him comfortable and overseer droids pulled up on speeder bikes.

"I'll get us out of this," she promised him. She didn't know how. She had no ship, and R2 was buried under a pile of scrap, but she'd find a way. . .

THE END

**CAN YOU GO BACK AND HELP LUKE AND
LEIA MAKE BETTER CHOICES?**

LUKE HAD HEARD ENOUGH. He closed his eyes and focused on the energy cuffs, reaching out with the Force. He might not have been able to push the escape pod from the *Falcon*, but he could disrupt a pair of binders.

Come on, he thought. *Come. On.*

With a click and the sound of sparking electronics, his wrists were free. He opened his eyes, raising his hand to call for his lightsaber when—

ZAP!

A beam of energy shot from the blaster in Craykan's hand. Luke was thrown back, skidding across the marble floor.

"Throw him to the scrap crabs," Yarla sneered as Luke was hauled to his feet.

Luke could barely walk as he was dragged away. The droids led him to a pit, which opened to reveal dozens of the crustaceans clambering over each other. While the crabs on the plains had been timid, these were crazed, with flashing cybernetic units fitted between their twitching eyestalks. The Tech Masters had experimented on the poor creatures, transforming them from peaceful scavengers to ferocious monsters.

There was nothing Luke could do. A metallic hand shoved him in the small of his back and he tumbled forward, falling towards the snapping claws.

THE END

CAN YOU GO BACK AND HELP LUKE AND LEIA MAKE BETTER CHOICES?

CAVAN SCOTT is one of the writers of *Star Wars*: Adventures in Wild Space and IDW Publishing's *Star Wars* Adventures comic book series. When he's not playing in a galaxy far, far away, Cavan has also written for such popular franchises as Doctor Who, Pacific Rim, Vikings, Star Trek, Adventure Time, and Penguins of Madagascar. You can find him online at www.cavanscott.com.

ELSA CHARRETIER is a French comic book artist and comic book writer. After debuting on C.O.W.L. at Image Comics, Elsa co-created The Infinite Loop with writer Pierrick Colinet at IDW. She has worked at DC Comics (Starfire, Bombshells, Harley Quinn), launched The Unstoppable Wasp at Marvel, and recently completed the art for the adaptation of *Windhaven* by George R. R. Martin and Lisa Tuttle (Bantam Books). She is currently writing two creator-owned series and has illustrated the first issue of *Star Wars*: Forces of Destiny for IDW.